A NOTE TO PARENTS

When your children are ready to "step into reading," giving them the right books—and lots of them—is as crucial as giving them the right food to eat. **Step into Reading Books** present exciting stories and information reinforced with lively, colorful illustrations that make learning to read fun, satisfying, and worthwhile. They are priced so that acquiring an entire library of them is affordable. And they are beginning readers with an important difference—they're written on four levels.

Step 1 Books, with their very large type and extremely simple vocabulary, have been created for the very youngest readers. **Step 2 Books** are both longer and slightly more difficult. **Step 3 Books,** written to mid-second-grade reading levels, are for the child who has acquired even greater reading skills. **Step 4 Books** offer exciting nonfiction for the increasingly proficient reader.

Children develop at different ages. **Step into Reading Books,** with their four levels of reading, are designed to help children become good—and interested—readers *faster*. The grade levels assigned to the four steps—preschool through grade 1 for Step 1, grades 1 through 3 for Step 2, grades 2 and 3 for Step 3, and grades 2 through 4 for Step 4—are intended only as guides. Some children move through all four steps very rapidly; others climb the steps over a period of several years. These books will help your child "step into reading" in style!

*With thanks to the Minnesota
Historical Society and the Orrock
family for sharing the story that
inspired this book —J. S.*

Copyright © 1995 by Joan Sandin
All rights reserved under International and Pan-American Copyright Conventions.
Published in the United States by Random House, Inc., New York, and simultaneously
in Canada by Random House of Canada Limited, Toronto.
Library of Congress Cataloging-in-Publication Data
Sandin, Joan.
Pioneer bear / by Joan Sandin.
   p.   cm. — (Step into reading. A Step 2 book)
SUMMARY: Andrew and his family are excited when a photographer comes to take a
picture of their dancing bear, but then Bearly can't be found.
ISBN 0-679-86050-9 (pbk.) — ISBN 0-679-96050-3 (lib. bdg.)
1. Photographers—Fiction. [1. Bears—Fiction.] I. Title. II. Series: Step into reading.
Step 2 book.
PZ7.S217Be   1995   [E]—dc20   93-48023
Manufactured in the United States of America   10 9 8 7 6 5 4 3 2
STEP INTO READING is a trademark of Random House, Inc.

Step into Reading

PIONEER BEAR

Based on a True Story

by Joan Sandin

A Step 2 Book

Random House 🏠 New York

Andrew found the bear cub
wandering in the woods.
It was crying for its mama.
The cub didn't know
what had happened to her.
But Andrew knew.
He had heard a shot.

Who could be so mean
to shoot a mother bear
with a cub? he wondered.

Andrew carried the cub home.

"What in heaven's name

are we to do with a bear cub?"

asked his mother.

"I'll take care of him," said Andrew.

"I'll feed him and teach him tricks."

"Tricks!" said his mother.

"Whoever heard of such a thing!"
But she didn't say
he couldn't keep the cub.
And so he did.

Andrew named the little cub Bearly.

He fed him warm milk

and corn bread soaked in honey.

He made a bed for him by the fire.

The little cub nuzzled Andrew's neck

and made snuffing noises.

He followed the boy everywhere.

Andrew taught Bearly

to stand up on his hind legs.

He even learned

to dance.

Thirty miles away,

a photographer named John Lacy

heard about the dancing bear.

"What a picture that would be!" he said.

He packed up his camera
and set off for the Irwin farm.

Hattie answered the door.
"Good day, young lady,"
said the photographer.
"I'm looking for a bear
that can dance."

"Bearly can dance," whispered Hattie.
"Who are you talking to, Hattie?"
asked her mother.
"My name's John Lacy, ma'am.
This here's my camera.
I wonder if I could take a picture
of your dancing bear."

Mrs. Irwin stared at the black box.

She had never seen a camera before.

"What will they think of next!"

she thought.

"Well, come on in, Mr. Lacy.

I'll send Hattie to fetch her brother."

Andrew stood by
the door and stared
at the stranger.
"Hello, son,"
said John Lacy.
"Do you know
why I'm here?"
"Hattie told me,"
said Andrew.
"Is that black thing
your camera?"
"It is," answered
John Lacy.
"Would it hurt Bearly
if you took his picture?" asked Andrew.

"Not a bit!" laughed John Lacy.

Andrew went outside.

"Bearly!" he called,

but Bearly didn't come.

Andrew looked for him in the barn.

Bearly liked to take naps in the hay.

But the little cub wasn't there.

James and Herman passed by

on their way to the root cellar.

"Have you seen Bearly?" Andrew asked.

He told them about Mr. Lacy.

"A <u>photographer</u>!" cried his brothers.

"Come on, we'll find that bear!"

"He's always sniffing
around the smokehouse," said James.
"Let's look for him there."
They saw some sausage and ham,
but no Bearly.

"He likes to nose around in the woods
for ants and honey," said Andrew.
"We could look there."

They found some nice ripe blueberries,
but no Bearly.
"Maybe he went fishing," said Herman.
"Let's look down by the lake."
But Bearly wasn't there either.

Jennie and Sarah were gathering vines
to make hoop skirts to put
under their Sunday dresses.

Andrew told them about Mr. Lacy.
"Oh, how exciting!" cried his sisters.
"We'll help you find him."

The girls looked in the outhouse,

behind the woodpile,

and in the chicken coop.

They found some fresh eggs, but no Bearly.

"I wonder what's keeping Andrew,"
said Mrs. Irwin.

She took a hot pan out of the oven.
"Mr. Lacy," she said,
"would you care to stay for supper?"
He smelled the steaming corn bread.
"I most certainly would!" he said.

Andrew spooned cranberries
onto his plate.
He poured thick hot gravy
over his chicken and potatoes.
He was glad his mother
had made such a good meal.

John Lacy wiped the gravy off his chin.

"A very tasty supper, Mrs. Irwin.

I thank you kindly.

I'm just sorry I missed seeing Bearly."

Andrew looked down at his plate.

He thought he might cry,

and he didn't want Mr. Lacy to see.

"I'll tell you what," said John Lacy.

"Since I've come all the way out here,

why don't I take a picture anyway—

how about a family portrait?"

"Oh!" squealed Jennie and Sarah.

"Say yes!" begged James and Herman.

"Please!" cried Hattie.

Mr. Irwin looked at his wife.

"That would be nice," she said,

"but not in our everyday clothes."

"Of course not!" cried Jennie and Sarah.

John Lacy looked out the window.

It would be getting dark soon.

"How quickly can you change?" he asked.

"Quick as a wink!" said Jennie.

What confusion!

It was like getting ready for church
on Sunday morning.
Mrs. Irwin brushed Jennie's hair,
Jennie brushed Sarah's,
and Sarah brushed Hattie's.

"I'm so glad we made hoop skirts!"
said Jennie.
"What if we had to have a picture taken
with our skirts all limp!"
"I'd sooner die!" said Sarah.

Andrew put on his itchy Sunday suit.

He laced up his stiff new cowhide shoes.

They hurt his feet,

but they were not hand-me-downs,

and Andrew was very proud of them.

"If only Bearly were here," he moaned.

He tried calling him
a few more times, but
Bearly didn't come.

John Lacy set up his camera.
"Bring out some chairs," he called.
"Hurry, the light will be fading soon."

Mr. Irwin sat down.

He was wearing his Sunday suit.

Mrs. Irwin sat beside him.

She was wearing her wedding dress.

It was a little tight.

Hattie climbed up on her lap.

John Lacy told everybody else
where to stand.

He put his head under a dark cloth.

"That looks good," he said.

"Now you must be very still.

Anybody who moves

will be a blur in the picture."

He slid the plate
into his camera
and took off
the lens cover.
He looked at his
pocket watch.

Andrew's nose
started to itch,
but he did not
scratch it.
He didn't want
to be a blur.

Finally, John Lacy said,

"All right, you can move now."

Hattie slid off her mother's lap.

Andrew scratched his nose.

Mr. Lacy pulled out the plate.

He packed it carefully

into his saddlebag.

"Don't we get to see?" asked Hattie.

"Not yet," he said.

"I have to develop it first.
Next time I'm out this way,
I'll bring the picture with me."

They watched John Lacy ride away.

Soon he was just a tiny dot on the road.

"When I grow up," said Herman,

"I'm going to be a photographer."

"Me too," said Andrew,

"a photographer—and a bear trainer."

Just then he heard a branch crack,

way above his head.

He looked up.

Something brown and furry
was looking down at him.
He could hardly believe it.
"Bearly!" cried Andrew.
"You rascal! Come down here!"

Bearly climbed down the tree.
He danced around Andrew
and licked his face.
"Now you do your tricks!"
said Andrew.

But he wasn't really mad,
and Bearly knew it.

Andrew watched every day

for John Lacy to come back,

but it was Hattie who saw him first.

"Here he comes!" she shouted.

"He must have smelled the corn bread!"
laughed Mr. Irwin.

John Lacy swung down

from his horse.

"I have a surprise for you," he said.

He held out a flat package.

"That's no surprise," said Hattie.

"It's our family portrait."

"That's true," said John Lacy,

"but it's also a surprise."

Everybody watched

Mr. Lacy unwrap the picture.

"Look!" shouted Andrew. "It's us!

And no one is a blur!"

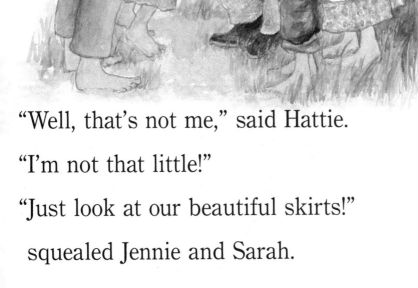

"Well, that's not me," said Hattie.

"I'm not that little!"

"Just look at our beautiful skirts!"

squealed Jennie and Sarah.

"Our house looks so fine,"

said Mrs. Irwin.

Her husband smiled proudly.

He had built the log cabin himself.

"What's that fuzzy thing?" asked Hattie.

"Up there in the tree?"

They all took a closer look.

There <u>was</u> something up in the tree.

Something blurry, and furry,

and brown...

Now Mr. Lacy was really laughing.

"I <u>told</u> you I had a surprise," he said.

"Bearly!" cried Andrew.

"That rascal was in the picture after all!"